SIMPLE SCIENCE

About this book

This colourful book encourages children to take an active interest in science. It stimulates them to observe things in the world around them, to ask questions and to think about what they notice. *Simple Science* aims to show that science is neither magic nor a specialist subject, but a fascinating part of everyday life. The book covers a wide range of topics and introduces children to the basic principles of physics by taking them step by step through simple experiments that they can do with everyday objects around the home. All the experiments are fun and safe to do.

Simple Science is written for children of 8-10 years old, but should appeal to older and younger children as well. Clear, simple explanations of basic concepts are given throughout the book, but no attempt has been made to explain everything, as explanations of some of the more complex principles might confuse rather than help young readers. At the back of the book there is a glossary, where children can look up the meaning of words which are new to them.

Simple Science aims to challenge and entertain children. Above all, we hope that it makes them want to find out more about why things happen as they do in the world around them.

First published in 1983
Usborne Publishing Ltd
Usborne House
83-85 Saffron Hill
London EC1N 8RT, England.

The name of Usborne and the device 🌂 are trademarks of Usborne Publishing Ltd.

Printed and bound in Great Britain

SIMPLE SCIENCE

Angela Wilkes
Illustrated by David Mostyn
Consultant: Alan Ward

CONTENTS

Science is all around you

Have you ever looked around you and stopped to wonder why things happen the way they do?

Being a scientist

You can be a scientist and find out things for yourself. This book is full of interesting experiments you can do at home.

How to be a good scientist

Look out for unusual things about everyday objects. Ask yourself what is odd about them and try to think of an answer.

Test your answers with careful experiments. Do each experiment more than once, to check that the same thing happens every time.

Science Notebook

Keep a science notebook. Write down all your experiments in it, step by step, saying what you did and what happened

Watch carefully when you do experiments. Draw what happens in your science notebook, so you have a record of your results.
If an experiment does not seem to work the first time you do it, try doing it again in a different way.

Don't worry if there are things you don't understand straightaway. Even famous scientists do not understand everything. There are always new mysteries to solve and new experiments to try.

Air is real

Air is everywhere. It is all around you but you cannot see it. Even things that look as if they are empty are really full of air. The only time you can feel it is when a wind or breeze blows, or when you breathe in and out.

Here are some things to do which show you that air is real and to help you find out more about it.

Hold a polythene bag open, pull it through the air to trap some air in it, then close it. You cannot see the air in the bag but you can feel how firm and squashy it is.

Now put bits of tissue paper on the floor and drop a book on them. The bits of paper blow away because the falling book pushes air out of the way and makes a wind.

The wind

Wind is moving air. Look for signs of movement in this picture. How many things can you see which show that it is a windy day? Do you think there is a gentle breeze or a strong wind blowing? Which direction do you think it is coming from? What would change if the wind stopped blowing?

The wind at work

People use the wind's force to make things move or work. The wind fills the sails of boats and makes them move along and it drives windmills' sails round.

Air not only has the strength to move things; it also slows down things that move through it. Try these experiments to find out how air can slow things down.

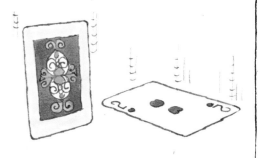

Wave a sheet of cardboard up and down. You will feel how the air pushes against it. Wave a bigger sheet of cardboard up and down. Do you notice a difference?

Stand on a chair and try to drop playing cards into a bowl on the floor. Drop some cards end on, and others flat face down. Which cards usually land in the bowl?

The red card acts like a glider and swoops to one side, but the air pushing up beneath the white card escapes fairly evenly all around it, so it falls straight down.

Why does a parachute come down slowly?

A parachute works in the same way as the card which you dropped face down. As the parachute falls, air is trapped under its canopy and pushes up against it. This makes the parachute fall to the ground slowly and land gently.

Make paper parachutes of your own like the one below. You can test them by dropping them from the top of the stairs, or stand on a chair to drop them.

Paper Parachute

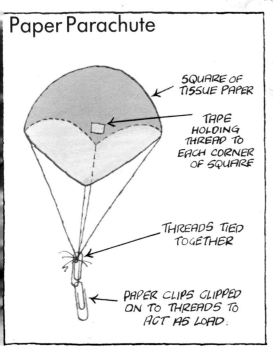

SQUARE OF TISSUE PAPER

TAPE HOLDING THREAD TO EACH CORNER OF SQUARE

THREADS TIED TOGETHER

PAPER CLIPS CLIPPED ON TO THREADS TO ACT AS LOAD.

Parachute tests

Test 1
Clip the same number of paper clips to a big parachute and a smaller one. Which parachute falls more slowly?

Test 2
Test two parachutes the same size but load one of them with more paper clips. What happens?

Test 3
Make a small hole in the top of a parachute and test it again. The hole allows the air trapped under the canopy to escape more smoothly, so the parachute wobbles less.

What happens to warm air?

Blow up a balloon. As you blow, the balloon's skin stretches and swells until the balloon is full of air and feels hard. If you blow any more air into it, it will burst.

Put the balloon in a very warm place, such as an airing cupboard. Leave it there for a few hours, then look at it. Why has the balloon burst?

Why the balloon bursts

The balloon bursts because the air inside it gets bigger and takes up more space as it gets warmer. Scientists say it expands. Air always expands when it is heated.

Hot air rises

Draw a snake like this on a piece of paper and cut it out. Hang it on a thread and hold it above your head. Blow gently up at it and the snake will spin round slowly.

If you hold the snake above a radiator it spins round again. What do you think is making it spin?

What happens

When you blow up at the snake, your breath makes it spin round. When you hold it above a radiator it spins round because hot air is rising from the radiator. When air is heated, it expands, becomes lighter than the cold air round it and rises.

Hot air balloons

Hot air balloons have hot air inside them. This makes them lighter than the cold air around them, so they rise off the ground.

A gas burner heats the air inside the balloon. The pilot can control the height of the balloon by turning the gas burner on or off. The balloon goes where the wind blows it.

When the pilot wants to land, he turns the gas burner off. The air inside the balloon cools down and becomes heavier and the balloon comes down to land.

Cooling down and keeping warm

Hot things cool down and cold things warm up until they reach the same temperature as their surroundings. If you leave a hot drink standing for long it tastes cold. Do this test to find out what makes hot water cool down.

Fill three bowls the same size with hot water. Put one bowl outside and the other two indoors. Blow on the water in one of the indoor bowls. Test the temperature of each bowl of water by dipping a finger into it

once a minute. Which bowl of water cools down the most and which one cools down fastest?

Hot water cools down until it is the same temperature as the air around it. The colder the air, the more the water cools down. It cools down faster if you blow on it, or if it is standing in a breeze.

Can you keep water warm? Fill two squeezy bottles with hot water and wrap one bottle in cotton wool. Which bottle of water cools down first?

In the second test the cotton wool round bottle B acts like a blanket. It traps air round the bottle and this helps to stop the heat from escaping so fast.

Trapped air keeps things warm

The pictures here show some of the ways in which trapped air can help to keep things warm.

Birds fluff up their feathers in winter to trap air and keep warm.

The air trapped in and between clothes helps keep us warm.

Wool feels warm because it traps a lot of air in its fibres.

Why do you think pipes are wrapped in soft material?

Bath water stays warmer if it has foam on top of it because air is trapped in the bubbles.

Duvets are light, but feel warm because there is a lot of air trapped between the feathers in them.

9

Vanishing water

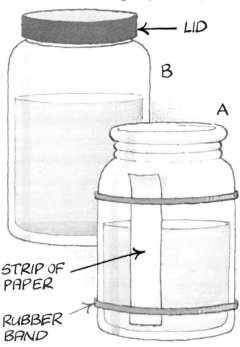

Puddle test

You can record how a puddle dries up. It is best to do it on a warm and sunny day. Find a puddle on a pavement or in the playground and draw a chalk line round it.

Draw around the puddle again every hour and you can chart how fast it dries up. Try doing it again on a cool, cloudy day. Does it make any difference.?

Jars of water

Find two jars the same shape and size. Fasten a strip of paper to one of them (A), as shown. Pour two cupfuls of water into each jar and screw a lid tightly on to jar B.

LID

B

A

STRIP OF PAPER

RUBBER BAND

Put the jars together on a window sill and leave them there for a few days. Mark the level of the water on jar A every day. What happens to the level of the water in jar B?

Water does not really disappear when it dries up. Tiny droplets of water rise into the air, but they are so small that you cannot see them and it looks as if the water has vanished. It has turned into water vapour. We say it has evaporated. The air is full of water vapour because water evaporates from oceans, rivers and lakes all the time.

Washing day

How and when is it best for Mrs. Bloggs to dry her washing?
On a cold day or a hot day?
On a wet day or a dry day?
On a windy day or a still day?
By folding the clothes or by hanging them up?

Do this test to find out

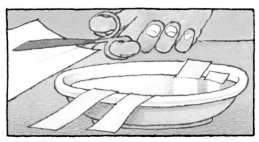

Find a bit of material, cut out six strips all the same size and wet them in a bowl of water.

Put one strip in the sun and one in the shade.

Hang one in a windy place and one in a still place.

Screw one strip up in a bundle and lay another out flat.

Which strips of material dry the fastest?

Water evaporates fastest in warm, dry places. Washing dries quickly on dry, sunny days and even faster if it is windy too. People hang clothes up because they dry faster if spread out.

Do you ever wonder why you feel cold when you come out of a swimming pool? Because you are wet, the water takes heat from your body as it evaporates.

Evaporating water always cools things down. When your body gets hot, it sweats and the sweat evaporates. This is your body's way of cooling itself down.

Athletes always put on warm clothes after competing. Even if they feel hot, they have sweated a lot and might catch a chill if they did not put on clothes.

Water from air

The water vapour in the air does not always stay there, but can turn back into water again. You can make water appear from nowhere. Put a glass of water in the fridge until it is cold. When you take it out, drops of water appear on the outside of the glass. Where do they come from?

The cold glass cools the air around it. Cold air cannot hold as much water as warm air, so the water vapour in it forms drops of water. This is called condensation.

On summer mornings grass is often wet with dew. At night the grass is cooler than the air around it, so water vapour in the air condenses and forms drops of water on the grass.

On winter mornings grass may be covered with frost. Frost is frozen dew. It forms when damp air flows across things that are below freezing temperature.

If you hold a mirror in front of you and blow on it you will see a misty patch made out of lots of tiny drops of water.

There is water vapour in your breath. As your warm, damp breath hits the cold mirror, the water vapour in it condenses.

On a very cold day your breath looks like smoke because the water vapour in it condenses in the air.

What is steam?

DO NOT PUT YOUR FINGER IN THE STEAM!

The same thing happens when steam comes out of a kettle. Water vapour coming out of the kettle cools down as it meets colder air. The droplets of water get bigger and you see steam.

The scientist in the bathroom

Where does rain come from?

The water that falls as rain does not just come out of the sky. It comes from the water around us.

The heat of the sun makes water evaporate from the sea and rivers all the time. The warm water vapour rises into the sky.

Fog is cloud close to the ground. It forms when the air is damp and the ground is cold.

When it reaches the cold air above the Earth, it condenses into tiny drops of water which join together to form clouds.

The clouds get bigger with more water vapour. Drops of water join together, become heavier and fall to the ground as rain.

If it is very cold it may snow. The water vapour in the clouds freezes into crystals and these join together to make snowflakes.

Strange effects with water

Water is a liquid and all liquids are fluid. This means that they have no shape of their own but move around easily and take the shape of whatever they are in, whether it is a pipe, a bowl, a bottle or a swimming pool. Unless liquids are put in a container, they spread out and run away. What do you notice about the direction in which they run?

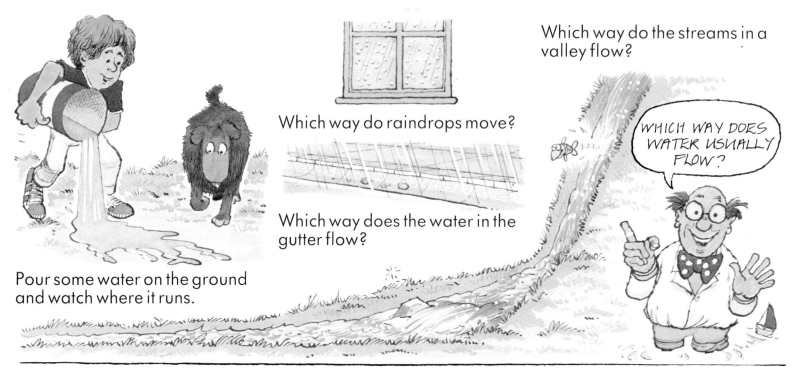

Which way do raindrops move?

Which way does the water in the gutter flow?

Which way do the streams in a valley flow?

WHICH WAY DOES WATER USUALLY FLOW?

Pour some water on the ground and watch where it runs.

Finding out about water levels

Find different shaped transparent containers and half fill each one with water. Draw a line on each container with a felt-tip pen to show where the water level is. Tilt each container in turn and draw the water level again. What happens to the water levels?

THESE EXPERIMENTS SHOW THAT WATER ALWAYS FINDS ITS OWN LEVEL

Do this test above a sink. You need a piece of plastic tubing and a jar of water. Suck some water into the tube and quickly put your finger over the free end.

Now hold the tube up like this and take your finger off the end. Move first one and then the other end of the tube up and down. What happens to the water level?

A magic trick

Suck some water up into a tube, quickly put your finger over the mouth end of the tube and lift the tube up, keeping it upright. All the water will stay in it.

But if you take your finger off the end of the tube, the water pours out of the other end. As air rushes in at one end, the water pours out of the other end.

Making a simple siphon

Fill a jam jar with water and stand it at the edge of a sink. Stand an empty jar in the sink itself so it is lower than the first jam jar.

Suck water up into a tube from the full jar until the tube is full, then quickly put your finger over the mouth end of the tube and put it in the empty jar. Take your finger off the end of the tube.

The water from the full jar will flow into the empty jar. When you remove your finger, water begins to flow out of the bottom end of the tube, but as the other end is in water no air can flow into it, so water flows in instead.

If you lift the bottom jar up above the top one while the tube is still full of water, the water will flow back the other way.

What happened?

Farmer Fred filled his horses' trough with a hosepipe from the nearest tap. When the trough was full he turned off the tap and unhooked the hose, but he left the other end of the hosepipe in the trough. What do you think happened?

The hosepipe acted like a siphon and all the water drained out of the trough.

15

Does water have a skin?

Do these experiments to find out something interesting about the surface of water.

A needle usually sinks if you drop it into water but it is possible to make one float on the surface of the water.

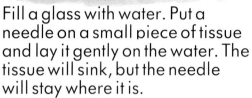

Fill a glass with water. Put a needle on a small piece of tissue and lay it gently on the water. The tissue will sink, but the needle will stay where it is.

Look closely at the surface of the water and you will see that it is dented all round the needle. It is as if the water has a kind of skin and the needle is resting on it.

Surface tension

The needle experiment shows that the surface of water is stronger than it looks and can support things. This strength is called 'surface tension'.

You can sometimes see insects called pond skaters skimming over the surface of a pond. They can actually walk on water because its 'skin', or surface tension, is strong enough to support them.

Bulging water

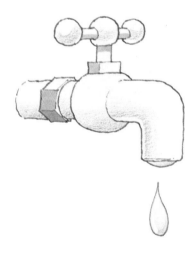

Now try this experiment. Fill a cup to the very top with water, then gently add a bit more, so that the water rises, but does not spill over the edge of the cup.

The water looks as if it is about to overflow, but it does not. Its surface tension is strong enough to hold it in place and stop it from overflowing.

Watch how water drips from a tap and look at the shape of the water drops. The water's 'skin' holds the drops together and gives them their special shape.

Is it magic?

Suck some water up into a straw and put your finger on the mouth end to hold the water in. Then release some drops of water on to a clean plastic tablecloth.

Look at the shape of the drops of water. Now dip one end of a matchstick into some washing-up liquid and touch each drop of water. What happens to them?

What happens

The surface tension of the water makes the drops of water stand up like buns. When you add washing-up liquid to the water, the drops spread out. This is because the washing-up liquid makes the surface of the water stretchier.

Blowing bubbles

When you blow bubbles, water really does look as if it has a skin and you can see how stretchy it can be.

Make a bubble mixture by stirring washing-up liquid into a cup of water. The washing-up liquid makes the water's 'skin' stretchier, so you can blow better bubbles.

Make a loop out of a bit of thin wire and dip it into the bubble mixture. You will see a thin film of liquid stretched across the loop. Now start blowing bubbles.

Blow gently, then harder, and the film of liquid will stretch. How big a bubble can you blow?

Are bubbles always the same shape?

Do bubbles change shape when they touch something?

Do bubbles bounce?

When do bubbles pop?

Do bubbles always float downwards?

Try blowing a stream of bubbles.

Floaters and sinkers

WHY DOES A BIG IRON SHIP FLOAT?

Pushing water out of the way

Next time you get into a bath, watch the level of the water and you will see that it rises. Try this simple experiment to find out what is happening.

Testing for floaters and sinkers

Collect lots of different things and test them to see whether they float or sink. You could test them in a large bowl of water, a sink or a bath. Make a chart showing which objects float and which sink. When you have tested everything look at the chart. Do the things which float have anything in common?

Things to test

needle
scissors
metal tray
empty tin can with a lid on
can of beans
plastic yogurt pot
dry bath sponge
wet bath sponge
cork
marble
ball of plasticine
ping-pong ball
wooden spoon
metal spoon
piece of wood

Water pushes back

Try to push a floater, such as a ping-pong ball, underwater and it always bobs back. You can actually feel the water the ball pushes away, pushing back.

Do things filled with air float or sink?

Try floating an empty bottle with its top on. Remember – the bottle looks empty but it is really full of air. Now take its top off and watch what happens.

Water pours into the bottle, the air bubbles out of it and the bottle sinks. The air inside the bottle was helping keep it afloat before.

Why things float

The more water something pushes away, the harder the water pushes up against it. A thing floats if the water pushes back strongly enough to support i

You need a wide-necked jar and two balls of plasticine, a big one and a small one. Pour some water into the jar and mark the water level on it with a felt pen.

Drop the small ball of plasticine into the water and mark where the new water level comes to. Take the ball out and do the same thing with the bigger ball.

You will now have three marks showing the different water levels. The water level rises when you drop a ball into it because the ball pushes away the water to make room for itself. The bigger the ball is, the more water it has to push away and the higher the water level is.

You can feel how water tries to push things up if you stand chest deep in a pool with your arms by your sides. Let your arms go and they will slowly rise.

If you lift a rock out of water, it seems heavier out of the water than it does in it. Things feel lighter in water because the water helps to support them.

You can have great fun trying to sink a floater, such as an airbed or an inflated tyre. How many people can sit together on an airbed before it sinks?

You can make a sinker like a ball of plasticine float by making it into a bowl shape. If the bowl does not float at first, try making its sides higher.

The plasticine floats now because you have made it bigger on the outside than it was before. It pushes away more water, so the water pushes back harder.

A heavy ship has to push away a lot of water to float. The bigger the ship is, the more water it pushes away and the harder the water pushes back.

19

Shadowplay

Why do things have shadows? Play these games on a sunny day to find out all about shadows.

Play catch with your shadows.

Does your shadow point towards the sun or away from it?

Make a monster shadow . . .

Can you jump on your shadow?

Why has the shadow disappeared?

Can you escape from your shadow?

Why things have shadows

Light rays are straight. When rays of light are blocked by an object, a shadow appears. Ask a friend to shine a torch at a wall, then try making different shadows with your hands.

Shadow puzzle

What is wrong with this picture? Look carefully at all the shadows.

The shadows of the boats' masts, the runner, the tree, the dog and the car are facing the wrong way. The boy's shadow is in the wrong place. The shadows of the ball, building and boat are missing.

Shadow theatre

Entertain your friends with a shadow puppet theatre one evening when it is dark.

Make puppets by cutting scary figures out of thin card and taping them on to thin sticks.

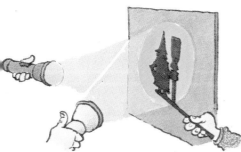

Hang a sheet across a doorway as a screen. The audience sits at one side of it and you and two friends on the other. One person holds the puppets while the others shine bright torches on them, to cast shadows on the screen. Move the torches backwards and forwards and watch what happens.

The nearer the torch is to an object, the more light you block and the bigger the shadow is.

If the torch is further away from the object more light can pass round it, so the shadow is smaller.

Making a shadow clock

Stand in a playground on a sunny morning and ask a friend to draw round your shoes and your shadow with chalk. Write down the time above your shadow.

Every two hours after that, stand with your feet in the same place and have your shadow drawn again. Write down the time above the shadow each time.

At the end of the day you will see that the position and shape of your shadow have changed. This is because the position of the sun changes during the day.

Reflections

Where do you see reflections? Collect shiny things – tiles, cans and bottles – and look at your reflection in them. When do you see the best reflections in water and windows? Look at your reflection in curved surfaces. What kinds of curves make things look thinner or fatter?

Mirror images

Look in a mirror and pull your right ear. Which ear does the image pull? A mirror reverses images from left to right.

Mirror code

Write a secret message to a friend in mirror code. No one else will be able to read it because it will be back to front.

Print the message on a piece of paper. Hold a mirror to one side of it and copy the reflected words on to another piece of paper.

Bouncing light

Reflections are caused by light bouncing off things. Try directing a beam of sunlight along a wall by reflecting it off a mirror.

Try this experiment. You need two cardboard tubes, a torch and a mirror.

Hold the mirror up near the edge of a table. Ask a friend to hold one tube at an angle to the mirror and to shine a torch down it.

Hold your tube next to the first one. Look through it and move it around until you see the light of the torch shining straight at you.

ook at your face in the bowl of a
oup spoon. Hold the spoon at
rm's length, then close up. What
appens to your reflection?

end this message to your friend.
o decode it, all he has to do is
old a mirror to one side of it, as
n the picture.

What happens

ook at where the tubes are, to
ee how the light moves. It shines
own one tube and reflects off
ne mirror and up the other tube.

Multiple images

Tape two mirrors together, stand
them up and put a toy between
them. How many images can you
see? What happens if you move
the mirrors closer together?

If you have two big mirrors, stand
them facing each other, then
stand between them. Look in
both mirrors and you will see
endless reflections of yourself.

A kaleidoscope

The patterns in a
kaleidoscope are
made by mirrors
reflecting off
each other. To
make a simple
kaleidoscope
you need three
mirrors the
same size, a
piece of white
card and bits of
coloured paper.

Tape the mirrors together, stand
them on the card and draw round
them. Cut out the triangle of card
and tape it to the mirrors.

Drop the bits of paper into the
kaleidoscope. How many
pattern repeats can you see?
Shake it to change the pattern.

Coloured light

Making rawbows

SUNLIGHT

WATER

MIRROR

WHERE DO THE COLOURS COME FROM?

Fill a shallow dish with water. Put it by a window in the sun and slant a small mirror in it facing the sun. Hold a piece of paper

above it and move the mirror until the sun shining through the water on to it is reflected on to the paper. You will see a rainbow.

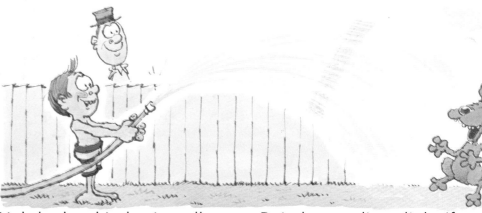

The colours you see in a rainbow are always in the same order. How many colours can you see and what are they? Where else do you see rainbow colours?

Light looks white but is really made of rainbow colours. The mirror and water split the light into colours and the mirror reflects them on to the paper.

Raindrops split sunlight. If you stand with your back to the sun, facing raindrops, you see a rainbow. Try making a rainbow with spray from a hose.

Disappearing colours

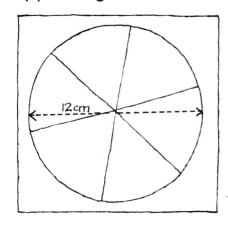

12 cm

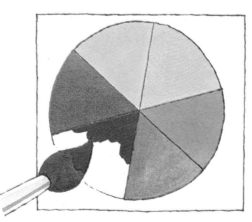

Draw a circle about 12 cm across on a piece of white card and draw lines across it to divide it into six equal parts.

Paint each part a colour of the rainbow in the following order: red, orange, yellow, green, blue and violet. Let the paint dry.

Cut the circle out neatly and punch a hole in its centre with the tip of the scissors. Push a sharp pencil through the hole.

Changing the colour of the world

Make coloured viewers to look through. You need card for the frames, cellophane in different colours and sticky tape. You can make window viewers or spectacles. Look through the viewers. What happens to the colours you look at? Which colours change the most? What happens if you overlap different coloured viewers?

The viewers are a type of colour filter. They only let through light the same colour as themselves, so they stop you from seeing some of the other colours.

Stained glass windows act like colour filters. They filter the light shining through them, as you can see from the patterns they cast on the floor.

Vanishing picture

This trick works well if you have a red pen and a viewer exactly the same colour. Draw a picture with the pen on white paper, then look at it through the viewer. Where has the picture gone?

Answer   The filter makes you see the paper the same colour as the writing.

When a colour wheel spins fast, your eyes see the colours but your brain cannot separate them and you see a different colour.

Spin the wheel fast and watch what happens. Which colour or colours do you see? Make different coloured wheels and

spin them. Make a chart showing the colour wheels and write under each one which colour you see when you spin it.

Spin a red and green wheel. Which colour do you see? Do you get the same colour if you mix green and red paint together?

25

Why do things make sounds?

MAKE YOUR OWN MUSICAL TOYS AND INSTRUMENTS AND EXPERIMENT WITH THE SOUNDS THEY MAKE.

WHAT A CAT!

Stretch a long, thick rubber band round an empty coffee jar and pluck the bit across the top of the jar. Why does it make a sound?

Look at the rubber band and you will see it shaking. Try the same thing with another rubber band. Does it also make a sound?

Plucking and pinging

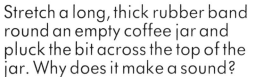

Stretch rubber bands round different things and pluck them. Do you always hear a sound? Do the rubber bands always shake?

What happens to the sound if you put your finger on a rubber band after you pluck it? Pluck the bands gently, then hard, to make soft and loud sounds. Do thick rubber bands make the same sound as thin ones?

Vibrations

When you pluck a rubber band, it shakes and makes the air around it shake. The air carries this shaking to your ear. Your eardrum shakes and you hear a sound.

This shaking is called vibration. Try these experiments to see how other things also make sounds by vibrating.

Sprinkle grains of rice on a drum. Beat the drum and the rice dances around because the drumskin shakes.

How sound travels

Make this telephone and talk to your friends through it. You need two yogurt pots and a long piece of thin string.

KNOT

Punch a small hole in the base of each yogurt pot. Push one end of the string through the base of one pot and tie a big knot in it. Then do the same with the other pot.

High sounds and low sounds

"YOU CAN PLAY TUNES ON THIS RUBBER BAND HARP"

You need a plastic box and eight thick rubber bands. Stretch the rubber bands round the box, then tighten them, by catching them on the edge of the box, to

give each one a different note. The tighter the rubber band, the higher the note it makes. Try tuning the rubber bands so you can play a scale.

Find some bottles the same size. Pour different amounts of water into them and tap them. How can you give a bottle a higher note?

Watch how musicians tune their guitars and violins by tightening the strings.

Hang a saucepan lid from a piece of string. Tap it with a spoon, listen and watch.

HHUUUMMMM!

Put your hand on your throat and hum a tune. What do you feel?

Hold a ruler down on the edge of a table and twang it. Does the sound change if you make the twanging end shorter?

For the telephone to work, the string must be pulled tight and not touch anything. Whisper into your yogurt pot while your friend holds his close to his ear.

Your friend can hear what you say because your voice makes the string vibrate and the vibration travels along it to the other yogurt pot. The sound of your voice travels better through the string than it does through air.

27

What is gravity?

Things do not move by themselves. They stay where they are unless something pushes or pulls them. When you kick a ball you make it go up in the air. But what makes it come back down to the ground?

The Earth pulls things towards it. This pull is called gravity. It makes the ball fall back to the ground, leaves fall from the trees and streams run downhill.

Weighing things

Make this spring scale and you can compare how much things weigh. Try to guess which things are heaviest before you weigh them.

You need
a yogurt pot
a thin rubber band
2 bits of wire both the same length
2 paper clips
a strip of white card

Punch two holes in the top of the yogurt pot and hook the bits of wire through them. Twist them together to make a handle with a hook at the top.

Hook the paper clips together and clip the bottom one to the card. Hang the rubber band from it and hook the yogurt pot on to it.

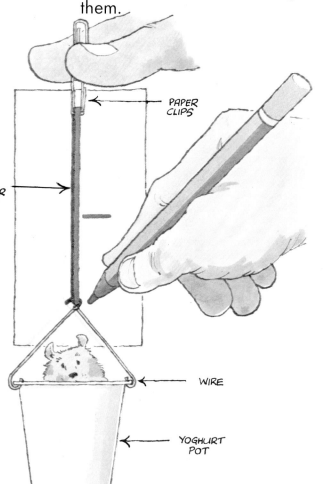

PAPER CLIPS

RUBBER BAND

WIRE

YOGHURT POT

Spring scales are often used to weigh wild animals. They are put to sleep first.

Put things in the yogurt pot to weigh them. Mark how far down the card the wire hook comes so that you can compare weights.

Things have weight because of the pull of gravity on them. The greater the pull of gravity on an object, the more it weighs.

A see-saw works like scales. How could the children help make the see-saw balance?

Gravity and movement

People often make use of gravity to make things move downhill.

Balancing tricks

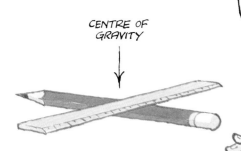

CENTRE OF GRAVITY

You can make a ruler balance on a pencil. At one point it acts as if all its weight were on the pencil because its two ends weigh the same and balance each other.

The balancing point of an object is called its centre of gravity. Try these balancing tricks.

Balancing Potato

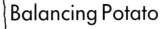

Push two identical forks into either side of a raw potato, as shown. Move them around a bit and you can make the potato balance on the edge of a glass.

Balancing a needle

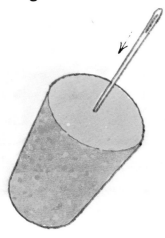

To do this you need a needle, a cork, a lump of plasticine and 20-30 cm of thin, stiff wire. Push the needle into the cork.

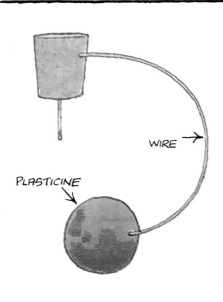

PLASTICINE

WIRE

Bend the wire into a curve. Push one end of it into the side of the cork and the other end into the ball of plasticine.

Stand the needle on the edge of a shelf. It balances as if by magic!

Bounces and springs

What makes a ball bounce? Where does its energy or 'go' come from? Bounce a rubber ball. How high can you make it bounce? How long does it carry on bouncing? Count the bounces and watch how high they are. Make a paper marker to help you measure how high the ball bounces. Drop the ball from different heights and ask a friend to mark how high it bounces.

Testing for bounce

Test different balls to see which one bounces best. Drop them all from the same height and measure the height of the first bounce. Make a chart showing how high each ball bounces. Which is the best bouncer? Look at its size and shape. What is it made of?

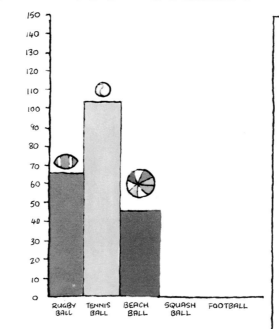

RUGBY BALL	TENNIS BALL	BEACH BALL	SQUASH BALL	FOOTBALL

Test your best bouncer on different surfaces — a hard floor, a carpet, grass and sand — to see where it bounces best. Always drop it from the same height to keep the test fair. Does the ball ever mark the surface? Does it still bounce well if this happens?

The plasticine test

Does a rubber ball's shape change when you bounce it on a hard floor? What happens when you drop a ball of plasticine on the floor?

All the plasticine's 'go' is used up when it splats on the ground. If you drop a rubber ball on soft sand its energy is used up making a dent in the sand. A ball bounces best when both it and the surface on which it falls keep their shape.

Energy from rubber and springs

If you stretch a piece of elastic and let go of one end, it springs back into place. You can use this energy to catapult things.

Springs can also make things move because they stretch, then spring back into place. Pop-up toys often have a spring.

A slinky *is* a spring. Make one move down some steps and watch how it stretches, then squeezes back together again.

Creeping toy

You need
an empty cotton reel
a candle
a rubber band
a matchstick
a thin stick about 10 cm long
scissors and a knife
sticky tape

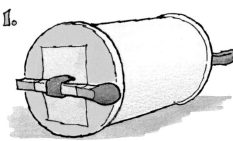

1.

Push the rubber band through the cotton reel. Push a bit of matchstick through the loop at one end and tape it down.

2.

Slice a ring off the end of the candle and make a small hole in the middle with the scissors.

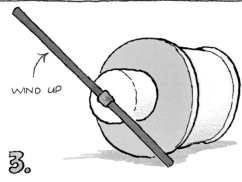

WIND UP

3.

Push the free end of the rubber band through the bit of candle. Push the stick through the loop.

Wind the stick round and put the toy down. It looks really creepy if you put a handkerchief over it.

How the toy works

The toy moves as its rubber band 'motor' unwinds. If you have a clockwork toy wind it up and watch what happens to its spring when the toy works.

31

Simple machines

For thousands of years people have made work easier by using machines to help them move heavy things. Make these simple machines and see how they work.

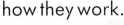

A lever helps you to lift heavy things easily. Make one by laying a short plank over a tin. Balance the plank so the lever has a short end and a long end.

Now try lifting some bricks with it. Put them first on the long end, then on the short end of the lever. When do you find it easiest to lift them?

A lever works like a see-saw. You can lift a heavy weight on the short end by pushing down on the long end. You do not have to push down with the same weight as the load, but you have to push further.

SHORT END

LONG END

If you have a strong plank and a thick, round stick you can lift a friend on a chair. Set up the lever as in the picture. Try lifting your friend by pressing down on the plank near to the chair, then further away. When is it easiest to lift the chair?

Levers round the house

Push the lid of a tin firmly into place, then try opening it with a coin. Now try again with a screwdriver. Which opens the lid more easily?

A door acts like a lever. It moves round the hinge. Try closing one by pushing it near the hinge, then near the handle. When do you have to push hardest?

A wheelbarrow is another type of lever and helps you to lift things you would not normally be strong enough to lift. The wheel acts as the balancing point.

Pulleys

When you use a simple pulley, you pull downwards to lift an object up, using your weight to help you. With a pulley like the one above you can lift an object which weighs as much as you.

Pulley puzzle

35 kl   50 kl   100 kl   150 kl

Mighty Max weighs 100 kilos. Which weights can he lift using a pulley like the one above?

What makes a crane so strong? Look at the number of pulleys the wire cable goes round.

Who is strongest?

Do this trick with four friends. You need two brooms and a long rope. Tie one end of the rope to a broom, then loop it from one broom to the other, as in the picture.

Ask your friends to try and pull the brooms apart, while you pull on the free end of the rope. Who is the stronger?

The brooms act like pulleys. The more times the rope goes round the brooms, the stronger your pulling power. The trick works even better if you dust the broom handles with talcum powder, so that the rope can slide easily.

Gears and pulleys

The chain wheel and rear sprocket of your bicycle act like pulleys connected by a belt (the chain). Why do you think they are different sizes? Study your bike.

How many turns does the back wheel make for every turn of the chain wheel? How many turns does the chain wheel make for one turn of the wheel?

Magnetic powers

Magnets attract things as if by magic. Do these experiments to find out about their strange powers. Use horseshoe magnets or, even better, bar magnets.

Which things are attracted to a magnet? Go round a room testing a magnet against different things.

Collect small objects, such as pins and paper clips and make a list of the things your magnet will pick up. Are they all made of metal?

Test the pulling power of your magnet. Can you pick an object up by holding the magnet just above it? What do you feel when you pull something off a magnet?

ARE MAGNETS ATTRACTED TO WOOD?

Does a magnet work through glass? Drop a paper clip in a glass of water. Hold a magnet against the glass and try sliding the paper clip up to the top.

Treasure Hunt

Put some small metal objects, such as screws and nuts, on a plastic tray and cover them with dry sand or sawdust. Use a magnet to detect where they are.

Magnet maze game

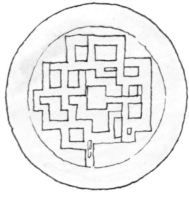

To play this game you need a bar magnet, a paper plate and a paper clip. Draw a maze or wiggly path on the plate. One person holds up the plate. The others take it in turn to hold the magnet under the plate and to try and guide the paper clip through the maze or along the path without touching any lines.

The poles of a magnet

Dip a magnet into a pile of paper clips. Which part of the magnet do the clips cling to? The ends of a magnet are called the poles. Are they stronger than the middle?

See if you can pick up a chain of paper clips with one end of the magnet. How long a chain can you make? What happens to it if you take it off the magnet?

Making a magnet

Hold the needle in one hand. Stroke it gently 10 times in one direction with one end of the magnet. Now see if you can pick up some pins with the needle.

Pushing and pulling

Try this experiment to see what magnets do when you put them together. Put two toy railway trucks about 2 cm apart on some straight railway track. Put a bar magnet in each truck and watch what happens. Turn one magnet round and repeat the experiment

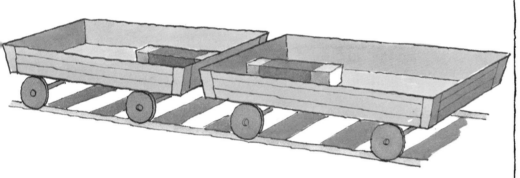

Hold the magnets close together and you can feel what happens. The two ends of a magnet are different. One end of one magnet attracts or pulls one end of the second magnet towards it, but its other end pushes it away.

Finding North

DID YOU KNOW THAT A COMPASS NEEDLE IS A MAGNET?

Float a bar magnet on a polystyrene tray in a bowl of water. The bowl should be big enough for the tray to float freely, so that it can find its own direction.

The tray will turn until one end of the magnet points to the North. A single magnet which can float freely, and which is not near iron, acts as a compass needle.

Crackles and sparks

There are two sorts of electricity: one that stays in the same place and one that flows through thing
You can make the first sort, static electricity, by rubbing things together. Do these experiments
and strange things will happen.

Magic Comb Tricks

Charge a clean plastic comb with electricity by combing your hair hard when it is clean. Hold the comb above your head.

Turn on a tap until there is a steady trickle of water. Hold the charged comb near the water and watch what happens.

Making sparks

Press a lump of plasticine firmly on to a tin baking tray. Hold the plasticine lump and rub the tray round and round on a big, thick plastic or polythene bag.

Lift the tray up and hold a metal object, such as a tin lid, close to one corner. You will see a spark jump from the tray to the tin, especially if the room is dark.

By rubbing the tray on the bag, you make electricity and when there is enough electricity it makes a spark. Static electricity builds up in clouds before a storm. Flashes of lightning are giant sparks of electricity.

Mrs. Brown cannot carry on with her housework because there is a power cut. How many things in the picture have stopped working? (Look for things that run on electricity).

It lights!

The electricity that is used to run machinery is called current electricity because it can flow through things. Find out how it works by making this simple circuit.

You need
a 4.5v torch battery
a 3.5v bulb and a bulb holder
3 pieces of single strand flex
a small screwdriver

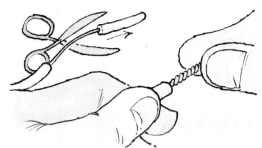

Cut about 2 cm of plastic from the ends of each piece of flex and twist the little wires together to make neat ends.

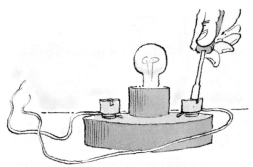

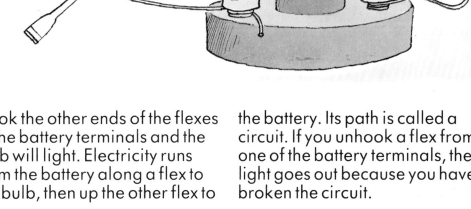

NEVER PLAY WITH ELECTRICITY FROM THE OUTLETS. IT IS **VERY** DANGEROUS.

Undo the screws of the bulb holder slightly. Hook the ends of two pieces of flex round them. Tighten the screws. Screw in the bulb.

Hook the other ends of the flexes to the battery terminals and the bulb will light. Electricity runs from the battery along a flex to the bulb, then up the other flex to

the battery. Its path is called a circuit. If you unhook a flex from one of the battery terminals, the light goes out because you have broken the circuit.

Does electricity only flow through wires?

Test different things to see if electricity will flow through any of them. Test lots of things and write down your results.

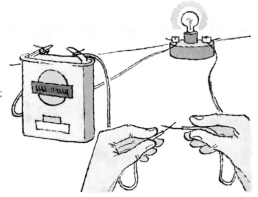

Use three pieces of flex for this test. Join them as in the picture. If you hold the two loose ends of flex together, the bulb lights, showing you have a circuit.

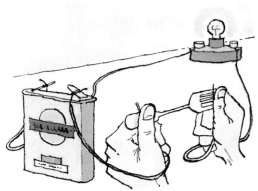

Hold the ends of each object you want to test against the two loose wires, as shown. If electricity can flow through the object, the bulb lights again.

Glossary

attract   Pull towards (p. 34).

centre of gravity   The point at which an object balances perfectly (p. 29).

condensation   Tiny drops of water you see on cold things. They form when water vapour in the air cools and turns back into water, or condenses (p. 12).

electricity   A form of energy that is easy to use. There are two sorts of electricity: static electricity, which stays in one place, and current electricity, which can flow through things (pp. 36/37).

energy   The 'go' in things, whatever makes them work (p. 30).

evaporate   Dry up and change into vapour that you cannot see (p. 10).

expand   Grow bigger (p. 8).

filter   A screen which only allows certain colours to pass through it (p. 25).

fluid   Runny, like water (p. 14).

gravity   The pull of the Earth (p. 28).

image   Reflection (p. 22).

kaleidoscope   A toy in which reflections from mirrors make patterns (p. 23).

lever   A straight bar which makes it easier to lift heavy things (p. 32).

liquid   A runny substance, such as water, which spreads out to fill whatever container it is in (p. 14).

machine   Any object that helps to make work easier (p. 32).

magnet   An object which can attract certain metals (p. 34).

multiple   Many.

poles   The ends of a magnet, where the power seems strongest (p. 35).

pulley   A grooved wheel over which a rope passes. It is used to lift heavy things (p. 33).

reflection   The light or image you see when light bounces off a surface (p. 22).

siphon   A bent tube used to move liquid from one place to another (p. 15).

transparent   See-through.

vibrate   Move quickly backwards and forwards (p. 26).

water vapour   The gas that water turns into when it dries up. It is made of droplets of water which are so small that you cannot see them (p. 10).